KU-199-033

A TEMPLAR BOOK

Produced by The Templar Company plc,
Pippbrook Mill, London Road, Dorking, Surrey RH4 1JE, Great Britain.

This edition produced for Parragon Books,
Unit 13-17, Avonbridge Trading Estate, Atlantic Road, Avonmouth, Bristol BS11 9QD

This book contains material first published as
The Noah's Ark Lion in Enid Blyton's Sunny Stories
and Sunny Stories between 1926 and 1953.

Illustrated by Sue Deakin

Printed and bound in Italy

ISBN 1 85813 523 0

POCKET LIBRARY

LION LEARNS A LESSON

Illustrated by Sue Deakin

PARRAGON

Sophie had a big Noah's Ark.
It was a splendid one, and
as well as Noah's family,
there were two of every
animal you can think of!

Lions, tigers, bears, horses, pandas, dogs, giraffes, elephants, ducks, chickens, pigs – there didn't seem to be any animal that wasn't there!

Sophie enjoyed playing with her ark. Every day she set the animals out in twos and made them walk into the ark with Mr. and Mrs. Noah. They liked this very much.

But at night the Noah's Ark animals had even better fun! Mr. Noah opened the door of the ark and let them all out to play!

S.H.D

They all tumbled out on to the ground and played whatever game they liked best. The ducks and hens played hide-and-seek, the giraffes played at racing, the elephants drew pictures, and the bears played leap frog. Mr. and Mrs. Noah and Shem, Ham and Japheth, their three sons, watched them and laughed.

When it was time for all the animals to go back into the ark they lined up in twos and marched in quietly. Then Mr. Noah shut the door after them and they all lay quietly in the ark without moving, waiting for the time to come when Sophie would open the lid and take them out.

Now all the animals were very good except the lion. He thought a great deal of himself ever since he had heard Sophie call him the king of the beasts. He wandered off each night by himself, for he thought he was too grand to play games with the others.

He sat by the fire and curled his long tail round him. Sometimes he nibbled a bit of the hearthrug. Sometimes he climbed up to the clock on the bookshelf and listened to its funny, ticking voice.

And when he heard Mr. Noah calling all the animals back into the ark, the lion turned up his nose and stayed where he was! *He* didn't want to go inside. Wasn't he the king of all the beasts? Why should he be hustled into the ark like the stupid ducks and hens and pigs?

Mr. Noah got very cross with the lion.

"Where's that lion tonight?" he would say. "He is just too tiresome for anything! Lion, lion, come at once! The other animals are all ready to march into the ark, and your lioness is waiting. Come at once."

But usually Shem had to go and find him and drag him to the ark. It was a great nuisance because it kept all the other animals waiting.

Now this happened night after night, and Mr. Noah got very tired of it.

"If you don't come when you're called tonight, lion, we shall march into the ark without you, and you will be shut out!" he said firmly.

"They won't dare to go without me," thought the lion to himself. "I shall keep them waiting as long as I please! Am I not the king of them all?"

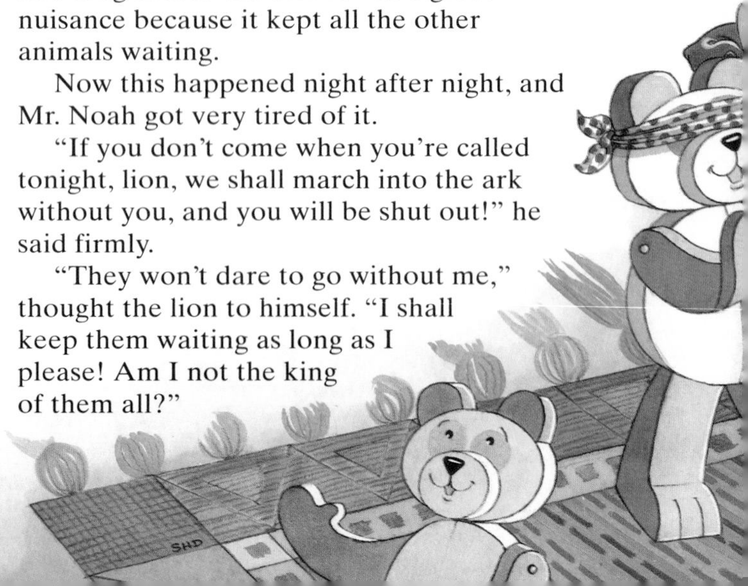

That night he sat himself down by the warm fire, curled his tail round him like a cat, and looked down his nose at the bears playing blind man's buff nearby.

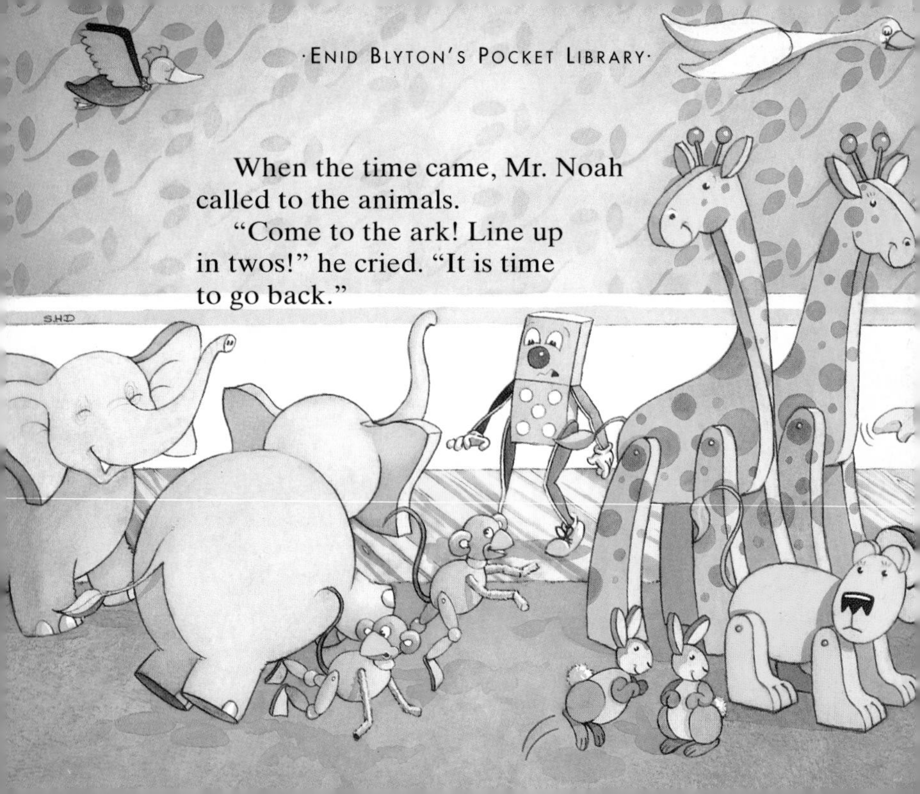

When the time came, Mr. Noah called to the animals.

"Come to the ark! Line up in twos!" he cried. "It is time to go back."

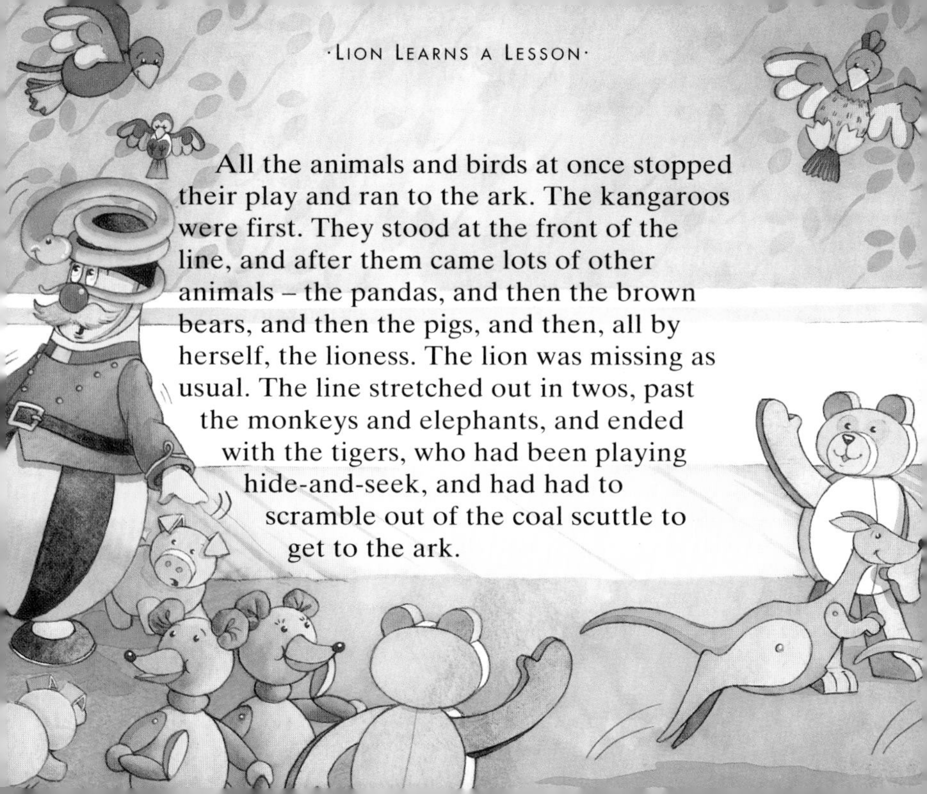

All the animals and birds at once stopped their play and ran to the ark. The kangaroos were first. They stood at the front of the line, and after them came lots of other animals – the pandas, and then the brown bears, and then the pigs, and then, all by herself, the lioness. The lion was missing as usual. The line stretched out in twos, past the monkeys and elephants, and ended with the tigers, who had been playing hide-and-seek, and had had to scramble out of the coal scuttle to get to the ark.

Mr. Noah saw that the lion was missing, but he said nothing. He didn't even look round to see where the lion was. He didn't tell Shem to go and get him. He just said,

"Shem, open the door. Ham, see that the elephants don't tread on the pigs. Japheth, tell the dogs to stop barking. Mrs. Noah, please would you be good enough to lead the way in?"

Mrs. Noah led the way. The animals went in two by two, except the lioness, who went in by herself. Mr. Noah went in last. He shut the door with a bang. Soon all the animals had settled down in the ark. Not a sound was to be heard.

Now the lion was rather astonished to see that all the animals had gone in without him. But he didn't say a word or even move from the hearthrug where he sat warming himself.

"I shall stay out as long as I like," he said to himself grandly. He looked round and saw that all the other toys were going into the toy cupboard. The dolls and the teddy bear always came out to play at night too. But now they were settling down quietly.

The teddy bear was surprised to see the lion on the hearthrug.

"Aren't you going to get into the ark?" he asked. "Won't you be frightened out here all alone?"

"Frightened!" said the lion, turning up his nose. "*Frightened!* Don't you know I am the king of all the beasts, and as brave as can be? What should frighten *me* I should like to know?"

"Well, if you feel as grand as all that, you can do what you like!" said the teddy bear in a huff. "I'm sure I don't care, Mr. High-and-Mighty!"

He went into the toy cupboard and slammed the door. The lion was now all alone. He sat on the rug and blinked at the fire. It would soon be out. The nursery was dark, but the lion could see quite well. He had eyes like a cat.

He sat there, and he sat there. Suddenly he heard a scratching noise in the wall nearby. He jumped to his feet. Whatever could it be?

It was the little brown mouse who lived behind the wall. He was coming out of his hole to see if the children had left any crumbs on the floor. He sidled out of the hole and ran over the hearthrug. He bumped into the lion and trod on his long tail.

"Ouch!" said the lion. "Why don't you look where you're going!" The mouse stared at him and grinned. He ran at the lion and bumped into him again.

S.H.D.

"I am the king of the beasts!" said the lion in his grandest voice. "So you'd better not do that again!"

"Well, you're sitting on a crumb," said the mouse. "And I want to eat it."

The lion sat down on the crumb and wouldn't move. He felt very angry with the mouse.

"I wonder if *you* are good to eat!" said the mouse suddenly. "Do you mind if I nibble your tail?"

"Yes, I do mind," said the lion who was suddenly scared. The mouse tried to get the lion's tail in his mouth and the lion ran away. The mouse chased him. He thought it was fun!

"I'll catch you in a minute!" squeaked the mouse. "And then I'll bite your tail!"

This frightened the lion even more. He ran to the ark and knocked loudly on the door.

"Let me in!" he cried. "A mouse is chasing me."

"The door is locked," said Mr. Noah. "And we are all in bed."

The lion ran to the toy cupboard, and knocked there.

"Let me in!" he cried. "A mouse is chasing me!"

"Go away," said the teddy bear sleepily. "You're waking us up."

L
H

Well, the lion would certainly have had his tail nibbled if someone hadn't come into the nursery on velvet paws and scared the mouse away. And that someone was the big tabby cat! She had smelt the mouse and had come after it.

The mouse shot into his hole. Then the cat saw the lion running and thought he must be a mouse too. So she went after him, and at last she caught him. She pushed him over and sniffed at him. He was very frightened. He felt sure she would eat him.

"You smell strange," said the cat. "Very strange indeed. You smell of wood and paint. I will not eat you – but I will play with you."

She began to push the poor lion about and throw him up into the air. He ran away as fast as he could and once more banged at the door of the ark.

"Let me in, let me in!" he cried. "A cat is after me."

"The door is locked," said Mr. Noah. "We don't want to be woken up."

Then the lion ran to the toy cupboard and knocked again.

"Please let me in!" he cried. "A cat is after me."

"Go away," said the teddy bear sleepily. "Do not wake us."

The poor lion did not know what to do – and then he suddenly saw the cat running out of the nursery door. She had heard a mouse downstairs and had gone to chase it.

The lion sat down in front of the fire again, tired and miserable. How he wished he was safely in the ark with all the other animals!

As he sat there a big spider ran over the rug and made him jump!

"Whatever's this now!" cried the lion. "Go away, whatever you are!"

"I'm going to spin a web from your nose to the leg of the chair," said the spider. "Keep still!"

S.H.D.

The lion gave a howl and ran away. He knew it was no use going to the ark. He knew it was no use going to the toy cupboard either. Where could he go to hide from all the mice, and cats, and spiders?

"What about the dolls' house?" he thought to himself. He ran over to it and pushed the front door. It opened!

The lion slipped inside, shut the door and went into the kitchen. He sat down in a chair there and sighed. At last he was safe!

He didn't feel brave now. And he didn't feel at all like the king of the beasts. He just felt like a very small and lonely and frightened lion.

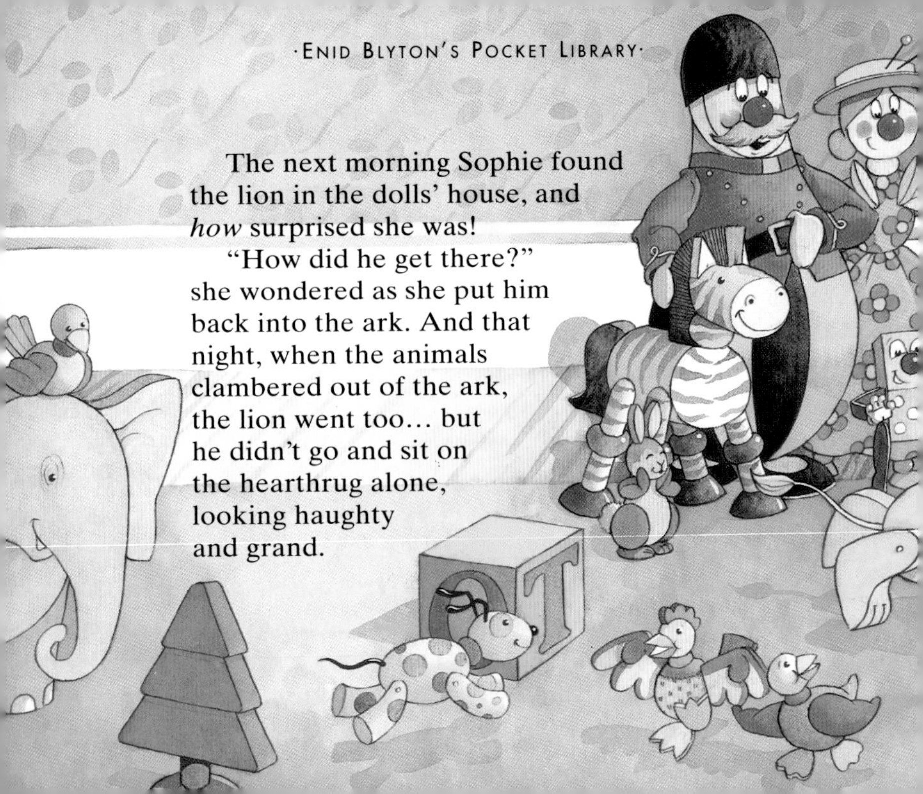

The next morning Sophie found the lion in the dolls' house, and *how* surprised she was!

"How did he get there?" she wondered as she put him back into the ark. And that night, when the animals clambered out of the ark, the lion went too… but he didn't go and sit on the hearthrug alone, looking haughty and grand.

No, he mixed with the others and played tag and hide-and-seek! And when Mr. Noah called the animals to him, who was the first one to come? Yes – the lion! He wasn't going to be locked out again! He had had enough of being grand and mighty. He just wanted to play with the bears and go into the ark with all the others.

The lioness teases him sometimes. She says,

"Who spent the night in the dolls' house like a doll? And who got chased by a mouse, and a cat, and a spider?" And do you know, the lion just goes red and doesn't say a word!